USED COW FOR SALE

USED COW FOR SALE

Poems of Love, Lust, and Lunacy

MELISA K. L. GRAHAM

Melisa Graham Creative
Fort Mill, SC

Used Cow for Sale: Poems of Love, Lust, and Lunacy
By Melisa K. L. Graham

Illustrations by Phillip Lewis

Second edition
Softcover, February 2024, ISBN 979-8-9899109-0-8
E-book, February 2024, ISBN 979-8-9899109-1-5
published by Melisa Graham Creative, LLC

First edition
Hardcover, March 2015, ISBN 978-1-943070-07-7
published by SPARK Publications

DEDICATION

For Todd,
who enjoys jump scares far too much

CONTENTS

I

The grass is the same color on the other side,
but try telling that to a stubborn, hungry, color-blind cow.

DOMESTICATED

The greatest barnyard debate
is the sum of one plus one.
One plus one equals always.
One plus one equals now.
One plus one equals breakfast.
One plus one equals two times two
   minus three hundred and fifty equals Vegas.
But cows, pigs, dogs, and cats
are generally bad at arithmetic,
almost as bad as people are at mending fences.

INTERSTICES

The void between
… then and now
… this and that
… him and her
… a rock and a hard place
full of crackle and promise and dread—
the dark matter that rounds the sum of daily life.
There the madness of all potential outcomes sits,
interstitially suspended
awaiting breath.

MARRIAGE COUNSELING

Walk inside and shut the door.
You put your right leg in.
You put your left leg in.
(You shake them all about.)
Then you shut the door.
Now clean the house.
Scrub it raw.
Scrub until your knuckles bleed.
Oh, bless, this house is so hot and dusty.
And we're so tired and thirsty.

Outside a spring shower blows gently in,
lobbing raindrops in slow motion,
hoping to meet our eyes and mouths,
waiting for its god-almighty right to be consumed,
watching and remembering we were born outside
where dirt is clean and lovely.

MISS ANTHROPE

Standing extra still, whispering
to an empty room.
Barely audible syllables fall
to the floor like mud,
reluctant to be known.
Others retreat down my throat,
to the cozy nook
in my toes
whence they came.
I'm counting off my thoughts in sighs
and guttural consonants
that form no words.

Standing extra still, whispering
to a crowd.
My elocutions buzz past
sooty, sweaty humans writhing
through a dusty town.

Asphalt-bound air
chokes the swarm
in this place.
No verdant hills
on which to land.
No creek nor vale.

Standing extra still, whispering
to the wind.
My dearest confidant,
he quietly cajoles
the secrets from me,
wrapping silky fingers
through my hair and
around my limbs,
kissing my eyelids
until my thoughts seem
soft and whole and finally utterable.

CREATION

I want to stand on the edge of a storm
in the warm but fleeting sunshine,
feel the heat prickle my skin and kiss my eyelids
as the storm wind builds.

I want the wind to blow my hair from my shoulders,
wrap his silky arms around me,
trail his fingers across my throat and down my back
before flying ahead of the storm.

I want the wind to take me with him.
I could stand very still and let him take me apart
piece by piece, cell by cell
until I'm down to my elemental self.
Then I'd be light enough to carry.

Then we could dance a new world into being,
like pale gods twirling naked across the sea.

THIRTY-SOMETHING

I scampered through my days

oblivious

as nameless vermin

gnawed holes in my shell.

Bits of me leaked out

dropping atom by atom

into thin air.

Now here I lie,

a half-empty sack of flesh,

the spaces within me aching to be filled.

DAPHNE'S CHOICE

She didn't want a man
so Daphne ran

became a tree
to keep virginity

but rhyming couplets
fall apart

without

the coupling

relaxed now in winter wind
unaware it's blown her bald
her hair dried and fallen
dragged to the nests
of countless fowl
Daphne sleeps
her snores, gentle creaks

come spring
come beetles
tickling, crawling
eating, mating
come birds and bees
and boys on knees

then we'll know
whether root-bound
freedom
suits her

II

—

*Why buy the cow if you've
never tasted the milk?*

SEVEN DEADLIES

My abundantly average body

holds sin in disproportionately large amounts.

I often marvel at the greed

that grows rampant in my belly at the sight of you.

I've raped you with my eyes more times than I can tell.

Surely you saw the salty lust spilling from them?

My fingertips envy the frail cotton touching your skin.

I'd sooner rip it from you than look at it another moment.

Pride fills my legs with rigid arrogance,

keeping them from wobbling when you look at me.

When finally I get my mouth on you,

I consume you in wrath for being made to wait so long

and in gluttony, not knowing when I'll get my fill again.

My higher faculties atrophy in sloth,

while my baser senses overflow.

And so I stand, horny and helpless, in my lack of contrition.

GREED

I first feel the need in my throat. And make no mistake—it is a need, not a want. I can skim over a want with naught but a sigh. But need takes hold before the sigh even passes my tongue, turning the breath to a pathetic whimper vibrating in some no-man's-land between my trachea and lips.

I try to ignore it, but need finds cunning ways to make itself heard. Soon the vibrato finds its way into my belly, disguising itself as water or some life-giving nutrient that is sucked into my bloodstream and into every cell of my body, mingling with my ribosomes, and whispering secrets to my messenger RNA.

It hums gently at first, almost pleasantly. But the hum builds to an exquisitely painful cacophony that drives logic and reason into the far, dark, quiet places of the brain where they can no longer influence action. And then what is left but to give in to need? Let it take me.

PUT ME IN YOUR MOUTH

Will I taste like
fresh turned dirt,
cut grass after rain,
or honeysuckle from the vacant lot?
Does it make your mouth water
to wonder?
I think you must taste like
carrots straight from my garden,
crunchy and sweet and mine all mine.

SUNDAY

I am supine on a blanket in the park,
shadows from an oak tree licking my toes lightly,
sunshine gently kissing my face,
breezes tracing cool fingers across my skin.
It isn't the orgy I dream of at night,
but it will do for today.

A HAIKU, MINUS ONE

Loose lips sink ships.
Your lips loosen my hips.
Undone, but one.

FIRST MATE

silky folds, warm and wet
pushing and pulling
to rhythm you set
greedy, silly folds
begging, "more ... no, stop ... yes, more!"
wanton, uncontrolled
silly fools are we
grinning, sleepy idiots
sailing inland seas

QUICKSAND

At first soft and cool and wet.

Why not sit back?

Enjoy a glass of wine while it sucks you gently under.

First your toes ... then your calves ... then your thighs and ...

oh, isn't that nice!

No need for alarm ...

... until it reaches your belly, where soft and cool and wet feel clammy and unpleasant. Panic sets in when it reaches your chest, and the crushing weight constricts your heart and lungs.

The urge to thrash about is uncontrollable.
But you mustn't.

Best to pour another glass of wine and lie back.
Rescue may come.
But if not, perhaps you'll die drunk and happy.

III

Neither look a gift horse in the mouth
nor eat chocolate found in a pasture.

DOWN THE RABBIT HOLE

He draws me down slowly
inch by maddening inch
through my own looking-glass
my pressed pleats and white gloves
stained and wrinkled
carefully twisted bun
coming undone
I'd trade my lucky foot
for tea out of time
for croquet with cards
instead of Him
always a few steps away
close enough to feel his grin
too far to win

YOUR TRUTH

The only truths I know float secretly from your lips in coitus.
The ohs and ahs that tell me
Yes!
There!
Don't stop!
Please stop! (But don't!)
Your eyes certainly tell no tales.
Your hands say only that they've traveled similar curves
Countless times before.

MODERN BULL

Spare me your spin
those twisted words and gestures
that point to this pile of shit
and say with faux gentility,
"Behold! Second-generation grass!"
I smelled your fecund turds
ere I saw them.
You can't fool me.
You jackass.

MY CLOTHING

Happiness is not a vestment I wear well.

My fatty regrets push at the seams

until they burst,

leaving only tattered smiles hanging from my limbs.

Then once again, I stand mostly naked and raw.

How else would you recognize me?

TIN WOMAN

I opened up my chest,
intent on scooping out my heart,
taking it to him, placing it on his lap
to show him how badly he broke it.
But when my fingers reached inside,
I found no solid muscle
pumping life through me.
My heart was mush.
I tried to gather it up in my hands,
hold my fingers tight to carry it.
But it oozed between my knuckles,
dropped in loud plops
to dusty ground.
By the time I reached him,
I had only half a heart left to show.

1000 STITCHES

The cuts went deep. Down to bone.

100 stitches across my forehead where I beat my head repeatedly against a wall in frustration and confusion.

100 stitches from ear to ear where lies left my jaw gaping open.

100 stitches on each shoulder, hand, and foot, where marionette strings pulled me into frenzied dances and finally ripped away.

100 stitches in my back where a dull, rusty betrayal
dug into my spine.

100 stitches across my chest where the rejection burned a hole
straight through to my lungs, letting all my air escape me.

I'll make a fine bride for Frankenstein.

UNEXPLODED ORDNANCE

I don't know what comes next.
I threw all my words at a problem
and watched them fall, ineffective.
They seemed as surprised as I,
their exclamation points twisting
into lopsided question marks
as they landed with a rough thump.
With my verbal arsenal spent,
I am strangely blank.
How lovely.
For me.

IV

—

Old cows can learn new tricks.

USED COW FOR SALE

My udders never worked well,

gave my babies sips of blood from cracked nipples

instead of gushing nutritious mucus.

So why buy the cow if the milk is free you say?

Mooooooot.

But I do have these sweet brown eyes

and wide bovine hips.

I'll look good in your pasture.

And I am completely full of verse-laden shit,

just right for your compost heap.

Buy me to help your garden grow,

and I'll greet you with a gentle low,

remind you of simpler days

when a man used his hands

to grow his food.

A WALK AFTER RAIN

The smell of damp earth greets me warmly as I step outside, as if to say, "Hello, my sweet. Where have you been? I missed you."

"Inside," I reply. "Locked away with my bitterness and regrets."

"That's no way to live," the earth tells me. "Stay with me. I'll heal your broken ego."

Clouds hanging low mute the sounds of birds and rustling leaves and cars. Only my own footsteps sound clearly in my ears. Dreamlike.

"Are you sure I'm awake?" I ask.

"Yes," she says. "Would you like me to pinch you?"

"No, thank you," I chuckle.

Water drips from leaves, making circles in sidewalk puddles. I step carefully around to avoid disturbing the concentric art.

I reach the park to find too many others with the same spring lust. Nervous parents letting their four-year-old ride his bike, barking commands at him when he goes too fast or gets too close to the water or into the mud. I stop and watch the geese awhile to let the gaggle of nagging humans pass.

The breeze picks up. Harbinger of more rain. I don't care. He's a balmy breeze who loves me. Any rain he brings will be a valentine.

On the road that leads back home, I hear distant church bells chime three o'clock. A misty rain begins to fall. It smells sweet and green. Feels soft and ticklish on my face. Sweetest of kisses.

LONG SLOW LICKS ON SKIN

The first time you touched me was with your eyes,
long slow licks over my skin while I walked toward you.
My nipples were the first to know we were done for.
When you kissed me, my breath and tongue colluded
to pull you in closer, to press your body against mine.
Your strength and warmth and smell wrapped me,
tugged me against gravity until I felt the pull in my core.
But that was just a taste of your power over my senses.
When you whisper in my ear, I can feel the soft vibration
travel across my back and down my spine to the tips of my toes.
Watching light play along your skin and chasing it
with my fingertips pulls me out of time.
When you lie above me and slide into me,
I can close my eyes and see my best self,
the one with no fears or worries.
When you pull me out of myself and listen to my chatter,
I forget that good girls hold their tongues
and remember that I don't want to be a good girl.
My tongue has much better uses than holding still.

When you care for me and I care for you,
I feel respected and fully deserving of it.
When you lead me on adventures,
I skip along in my head, though my body
rebels against the unaccustomed strain.
Touch me, love, inside and out.

DANCING WITH A SUNBEAM

Lilting notes settled in my ears
while my mind was turned inward.
I began dancing even before
I was aware of any song,
turning and turning on my tippy toes
until I collapsed, laughing and out of breath.
And then the world spun away,
taking up my turns and the tune.

HEAVY

Carrying these words around
somewhere near my diaphragm,
their three short syllables belie
their weight on my belly.
Why dig them out and drop them
on such a perfect moment?
Their weight could crush this tender thing.

HINDSIGHT

Take that thought and bottle it up.

You know the one I mean—

either the one you're afraid to say aloud

or the one you think shouldn't be given breath.

Wrap the bottle in seven layers of brown paper.

Tie it up with pretty ribbon,

maybe ridiculous ribbon, with hot pink polka dots.

Maybe let it sit under your Christmas tree, year after year,

a present for your future self.

Then bury it in a box in the farthest corner of your attic.

Let it gather dust for a decade.

Maybe two.

Then one day, perhaps during a move,

perhaps just because—

find it.

Maybe shed a tear for your oldest friend (you),

who sealed away such a thing,

who was afraid of such a thing.

BENEDICTION

They say if you love something,
you should set it free.
Well, I love these words you said to me:
My skin looks good next to yours;
I should wear you every day.
Yes, my love, you should.
And accessorize with the kisses
I'll give you down your neck,
over your hip bone,
and on that sweetest spot
that always rises to my whim.
Now fly away, sweet words.
Live, grow, and multiply.

DEAR READER

The first edition of this chapbook came during a very different season in my life. While I wrote at least one of the poems as a teenager, most of them came to me during a period of drastic change: divorce, separation, single motherhood, and then reentering the dating scene as a thirty-something-year-old woman. Dating was extra shocking for me because I'd married so young, nineteen and still in college, that I'd never been on a first date with an adult before. My mistakes were many and varied, though I do have a few fond memories of trying on different versions of myself to see what fit.

Then I got a message on Match.com from Todd. He used ellipses extravagantly, wantonly even, so initially I thought we couldn't possibly be a good match. But he won me over when his message dispensed with small talk and delved right into the important issues: he asked me to rank a list of foods in order from best to worst. We agreed that chips and salsa are #1, and I convinced him to give sushi another try.

After dating and then cohabitating for five years, we were about to get married, my second marriage and his third. Except for his eldest son who was in his twenties and lived far away, our children ranged in age from eleven to fourteen. Our lives were filled with the daily dramas and traumas of the kids' middle and high school lives, our full-time jobs, and coparenting with our former spouses. The books came in just in time to gift a copy to each of our moms on the weekend of our wedding.

Much has changed since then. We've watched our children struggle through mental health challenges, heartbreak, a pandemic, and emerging adulthood. His mother passed away. A year later, he developed a potentially life-threatening neurological disorder. Perimenopause hit me hard. I stopped sleeping and journaling and generally giving a shit. I quit my job in a burnout haze and started freelancing from home while I tried to force my body and mind to cooperate with me. Several diagnoses and medication adjustments later, I'm learning to cooperate with my changing body and mind. Me, myself, and I frequently disagree on what that means.

Amidst the uncertainty, an old friend, Cindy Urbanski, issued an invitation to participate in a collaborative book called *Unveiling the Secrets: An Encyclopedia By Women for Women (and Those Who Love Them)*. While I write and edit for a living, I'd neglected my personal creative writing for a long time. I joined the writing group and contributed three essays, which felt really good.

The writing group's lead, Shana Hartman, suggested I publish a second edition of *Used Cow for Sale* and start working on a new book. Or maybe it was the other way around. I'm not sure which is the horse and which the wagon. Anyhoo, I'm doing both. I'm not sure when the new book will be ready or even what it's final form will be. More poetry? Essays? Letters to my imaginary friends? All of the above? I guess we'll find out together.

I would like to thank Cindy and Shana for the nudges they've given me to keep putting my work out there; Brian Francis for the nudges he gave me to create the first edition of this book; Fabi Preslar and SPARK Publications for producing and publishing the first edition, which is still available from my website as a *beautiful* hardcover if you're feeling nostalgic; Genna Hardgrove who designed the first edition (the second edition mimics the original); Alice Osborn and Wendy H. Gill who edited the first edition; Joe Miller who helped me produce the first edition audiobook (yep, you can listen to me read these); Phillip Lewis for his artwork and continued friendship; my kids and parents for consistently hyping my creative endeavors; and Todd Graham for a ridiculously long list of reasons.

Most especially, I would like to thank you, dear reader, for picking up this sexy little chapbook and giving it your time. I hope you enjoyed it. If you didn't, oh, dang, sorry about that. Either way, I'd love your honest review on Amazon or the review platform of your choice. And, please, let's keep in touch. Connect with me on Instagram and Threads @1smelisa and join my email list at melisagrahamcreative.com/sign-up.

YOURS IN LOVE AND LUNACY, MELISA

ABOUT THE AUTHOR

Melisa K. L. Graham was born and raised in Charlotte, North Carolina, to a family with its roots deeply embedded in the North Carolina mountains. Her childhood weekends were split between church activities and visiting the family farm. On those trips to the hills, she learned never to pass a pasture without mooing at the cows. It's rude not to say hello to your neighbors. And what is life if you can't make weird noises when the spirit moves you?

She earned her bachelor's degree from Duke University with a double major in English and religion. Most of her English classes had religious themes, and most of her religion classes had literary themes.

She currently works as a freelance writer, ghostwriter, and editor. Her work (at least the bits with her own byline) has appeared in *Kakalak 2013*, *b2bTRIBE* magazine, and *Unveiling the Secrets*. Connect with her on Instagram and Threads @1smelisa.

ABOUT THE ILLUSTRATOR

Phillip Lewis grew up in Fayetteville, North Carolina, and developed an early appreciation for art from his parents, who were both teachers. He attended Appalachian State University, where he earned a bachelor's degree in communications, and upon graduating moved to Charleston, South Carolina, putting his degree to good use as a bartender and beach bum. After many years of slinging drinks, he moved to Charlotte and joined the corporate world as a web developer. Phillip is part of an improv group that performs in and around the Charlotte area to dozens of people, none of whom have ever asked for a refund. Phillip is an avid indoor enthusiast and enjoys relaxing on the couch watching cartoons and anything that might have elves, dwarves, swords, and/ or dragons in it. Lightsabers will also do the trick. Connect with him on Instagram at @jager2ways.